E
EMB

Emberley, Michael.
Ruby and the Sniffs.

$15.95

000044501
12/24/2004

DATE			

RUBY
and the
Sniffs

Also by Michael Emberley:
Ruby
Three: An Emberley Family Sketchbook
Dinosaurs! A Drawing Book

RUBY
and the
Sniffs

Michael Emberley

LITTLE, BROWN AND COMPANY

New York ⌁ An AOL Time Warner Company

For Ruby's most loyal friend, John Keller

*T*HUMPITY BUMP!

"Listen!" Ruby whispered, looking up.

"I'm reading," said Mrs. Mastiff.

BUMPITY THUMP!

"Hear that?" Ruby's eyes narrowed. "It's *cat burglars!*"

"No, it isn't," said Mrs. Mastiff. "This is a cat-free building."

"Let's go upstairs and see!" said Ruby.

"No. Let's not," said Mrs. Mastiff.

Ruby rolled her eyes, then stared at the ceiling for a while, listening and thinking.

"Let's play a game," she said. "Hide-and-seek. I hide. You seek."

Mrs. Mastiff put her book down and peered over her glasses at Ruby. "Very well," she said. "But hallways and stairs are off-limits."

Ruby nodded her head. "Okeydokey."

"That means stay in the apartment...agreed?"

Ruby nodded again. "You betcha."

"Good. I'll give you to twenty. Ready?"

Ruby grinned. "I was *born* ready."

Mrs. Mastiff started to count.
"ONE!...TWO!...THREE!..."
Ruby was off like a shot to the kitchen.

"FOUR!...FIVE!...SIX!..."
Ruby carefully opened the back door
and slipped out.

"SEVEN!...EIGHT!...NINE!..."
Ruby closed the door and was
zooming up the hall stairs before
Mrs. Mastiff could count to ten.

Ruby sprinted down the hall carpet to the apartment just above her own. The door was open a crack. "Aha!"

Ruby tapped on the door. No answer.

She whispered, "Hello? Any burglars in here?"

Ruby crept inside. "Anybody home?" she said. "This is Ruby, the crook-catcher. All burglars come out and give yourselves up!" She had a look around. But there was nobody there. No burglars. No bumps. Just boxes. And a funny smell. Ruby's nose wrinkled.

The place smelled like a pig pen.

Suddenly, there was a noise in the hallway. Ruby's whiskers shot out. Someone was coming.

From the other room, she heard the front door creak open, and then muffled grunting sounds.

Ruby dashed to the next room and shut the door. There were three beds in the room. Quick as a blink, Ruby dove under the first one — but it was too high to hide her. *Bats biscuits!*

Frantically, she tried squeezing under the second bed — but it was too low. *Rats rickets!*

She fit under the third bed perfectly, but then —*KA-CLUNK!*— two legs fell off. Ruby froze. The grunting stopped. Then she heard a sound that gave her goosebumps from tail to snout.

It was *sniffing.*

The sniffing came closer. Ruby covered her eyes. She heard the door open. The sniffing grew louder and louder. Then she felt hot, smelly sniffing on her fur.

Ruby couldn't stand it. She opened her eyes and found herself nose-to-nose with three of the biggest snouts she had ever seen.

"Yikes!" shrieked Ruby.

"Yikes!" shrieked the snouts.

"Stop sniffing me!" Ruby shouted. Leaping up, Ruby discovered that the three enormous snouts were attached to three enormous pigs.

"Look!" squealed the littlest enormous pig. "A gerbil! A gerbil!"

Ruby straightened up.

"Listen, Porkchop," she snapped, "I am *no* GERBIL!"

"Holy hogwash!" bellowed the biggest enormous pig. "Whatever you are, you darn near scared the ham hocks off us!"

Ruby stood as tall as she could. "My name is Ruby, bacon-breath. I live downstairs. Who are *you*?!"

"Who are we? Who are we? Why, we're the Sniffs, of course! Always have been!"

"Sniffs?" said Ruby, wondering what the reward would be for three very loud, enormous pig burglars.

"Sure! I'm Biff Sniff, but call me Poppa. This is Momma Sniff, and the little one's Baby Sniff!"

Baby Sniff danced around in a tizzy. "Can we keep the gerbil, huh, Momma?! Can we?! Huh?! Can we?!"

"Hush, Baby!" scolded Momma Sniff. "Rats don't like being called that."

Ruby gritted her teeth. "What are you 'Sniffs' doing in here?!"

"What are we doin' here? We live here! Just moved in!"

"Uh-oh," thought Ruby.

"And what are you doing here?"

"Me? . . . I, uh . . . I was looking for burglars."

"BURGLARS!?" shrieked the Sniffs. "Where!?"

"No, no!" said Ruby. "I thought *you* were the burglars."

Momma Sniff chuckled. "That's silly, dear," she snorted. "We're not burglars! We're Sniffs! Always have been!"

Poppa Sniff slapped his belly. "Frizzle my bristles!" he roared. "You must've scared them burglars off!" He gawked at Ruby. "Well twist my tail and call me a guinea pig! Boy, you're a HERO!"

Baby Sniff sang, "Baby keep the gerbil! Baby keep the gerbil!"

"I am *NOT* a gerbil!" Ruby yelled. "I am not a *rat,* and I am *NOT* a BOY!"

"Don't get your tail in a twist, son," said Poppa Sniff. "I take it back. You sure did a real *man's* job today!"

"Say, where's my Sniff manners?! Baby! Stop flappin' yer gums a minute and offer our resident rodent here a seat!" Baby Sniff clunked Ruby into a big chair.

"Not my chair!" shouted Poppa Sniff. "It's too hard!"

Baby Sniff flopped Ruby into a medium chair.
"Not my chair, dear," snuffled Momma Sniff. "It's
too soft."

"Mine!" squealed Baby Sniff, jumping with Ruby onto a small chair and smashing it to pieces. "Jus' right!" squealed Baby Sniff.

"I fink I meed o goo hmm new," Ruby moaned.

"You must be one hungry hamster after all that burglar hunting!" bellowed Poppa Sniff. "And I got just the thing!" He stopped and glowered at a plate. "Gnat's knuckles! Somebody's been eating the pickled potato peels!"

"They were so nice and moldy, too," said Momma Sniff. "And look! Someone's been nibbling the slippery gristle!"

"Slippery gristle! Slippery gristle!" Baby Sniff chanted, spinning around.

"And *somebody*," snorted Poppa Sniff, "has been eating my sticky fish heads!" He looked around suspiciously. "And they ate them all up!"

"All up!" shrieked Baby Sniff.

"I really think I need to go home now...," said Ruby.

BANG BANG!
The noise froze everyone in their tracks.

"BURGLARS!!" squealed the Sniffs.

Ruby rolled her eyes. "Pigs," she muttered. "There *are* no burglars. It's just someone at the door." Ruby went to open it.

"Not that door, dear," said Momma Sniff. "That's the closet."

But it was too late . . .

Cat fur, coat hangers, and the powerful odor of rotten fish exploded out of the closet.

"B-B-BURGLAR!!" croaked Ruby. "*Real* burglar!"

There were squeals and grunts and squeaks as three pigs and one mouse scattered in every direction.

"Cat burglar!" screeched Momma Sniff.

"Kitty burglar!" squealed Baby Sniff.

"My fish heads!" yelled Poppa Sniff.

Ruby saw the cat burglar bolting for the door.

"STOP THAT CAT!!"

Suddenly, like a locomotive out of a tunnel, a large, well-dressed baby-sitter charged through the doorway, halting the intruder with a perfectly timed linebacker tackle.

"Sorry to disturb you," said Mrs. Mastiff politely, looking up from the floor. "But I was looking for Ruby."

"You must be Mrs. Ruby!" said Momma Sniff. "We're the Sniffs!"

"My name's Edna," said Mrs. Mastiff. "How do you do?"

"Nice tackle, Ed!" said Poppa Sniff, sitting down. "I'm Biff. Biff Sniff. You play football?"

"Somebody call nine-one-one!" shouted Ruby.

"That's a good idea!" said Momma Sniff. "What's the number?"

Ruby sighed, rolled her eyes, went to the phone, and punched the number.

"Hello? Nine-one-one? I want to report a cat burglar stealing fish.... The Sniffs.... That's right, three pigs, two F's.... Forty-two Cheddar Street, top floor.... Yup, like the cheese.... No. No trouble. ... Uh-huh, tackled.... My baby-sitter.... Yeah, big baby-sitter. Okay, ten-four, over and out."

"Fifteen minutes to cop time," said Ruby.

"Holy hedgehog, son!" said Poppa Sniff. "That was just like on TV!" He stuck out a hoof. "You are truly *one stinkin' rat!*"

Ruby held out her paw. "And you, sir, are one stinkin' pig."

Poppa Sniff peered at Ruby for a moment. "Why, thank you, son. That's mighty piggish of you."

"Okay, pig party's over," Ruby announced. "We gotta go. Ready, Ma?" Mrs. Mastiff gave Ruby a look.

"Gerbil go home?!" asked Baby Sniff.

"Goodbye, dear," said Momma Sniff, giving Ruby a big, bristly kiss. "Thank you both for saving our fish heads."

"Thanks for everything, Ed," said Poppa Sniff, slapping Mrs. Mastiff on the back. "We'll show kitty here some real Sniff hospitality until the law shows up, don't you worry."

The Sniffs all waved. "Don't be strangers!"

As the door closed, Ruby could hear Baby Sniff pleading, "*Please,* Poppa?! Can we keep the kitty?! Can we?! *Pleeeease?!*"

"You found me," said Ruby.

"Yes, I did," replied Mrs. Mastiff.

"I said it was a burglar, didn't I?!"

Mrs. Mastiff sighed. "Yes, you did. You also said you wouldn't leave the apartment."

"Yes, I did." Ruby looked at the carpet. "Did I say I was really, really sorry and promise never to do it again?"

"Yes," said Mrs. Mastiff quietly, "you just did."

"Any crook-catchers I know ready for lunch?" asked Mrs. Mastiff.

"Ready? I was *born* ready!"

Ruby took Mrs. Mastiff's big paw and headed down the stairs. "Make mine toasted cheese, please! Easy on the slippery gristle, and *pleeeease* hold the fish heads!" Ruby's nose wrinkled. "You know, *Ed,* you *smell* a little like fish heads."

"Why, thank you, *son,*" said Mrs. Mastiff. "That's mighty piggish of you."

First Edition

Library of Congress Cataloging-in-Publication Data

Emberley, Michael.
Ruby and the Sniffs / written and illustrated by Michael Emberley. — 1st ed.
p. cm.
Summary: Ruby the mouse investigates the possibility of burglars in the upstairs apartment,
but finds some generous but overwhelming new neighbors instead.
ISBN 0-316-23664-0
[1. Mice — Fiction. 2. Pigs — Fiction. 3. Neighbors — Fiction. 4. Apartment houses — Fiction.
5. Humorous stories.] I. Title.

PZ7.E566 Rv 2003
[E] — dc21   2001038309

10 9 8 7 6 5 4 3 2 1

TWP

Printed in Singapore

The illustrations for this book were done in colored pencil, watercolor, and dry pastel
on 90-lb. hot-press watercolor paper.
The text was set in Minion, and the display fonts are Showcard Gothic and Chiller Plain.